DYLAN
The Eagle-Hearted Chicken

by David L. Harrison

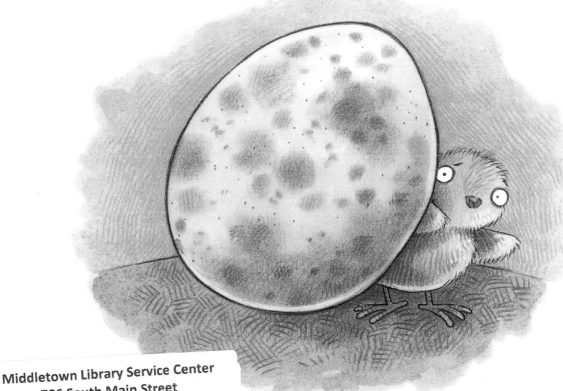

Illustrated by Karen Stormer Brooks

To Wanda Gray,
who has taught so many
how to serve children.
—D. L. H.

For Connor and Holly, and especially Scott
—K. S. B.

Published by Boyds Mills Press, Inc.
A Highlights Company
815 Church Street
Honesdale, Pennsylvania 18431
Printed in China
Visit our Web site at www.boydsmillspress.com

Publisher Cataloging-in-Publication Data (U.S.)

Harrison, David L.
Dylan the eagle-hearted chicken / by David L. Harrison ; illustrated by Karen Stormer Brooks. — 1st ed.
[32] p. : col. ill. ;   cm.
Summary: As a chicken egg, Dylan is placed in an eagle's nest and when he hatches, confuses himself—
and others—about what kind of bird he really is.
ISBN 1-56397-982-9
1. Chickens—Fiction. 2. Eagles—Fiction. I. Brooks, Karen Stormer. II. Title.
[E]   21   2002   AC   CIP
2001094537

First edition, 2002
The text of this book is set in 15-point Optima.

10 9 8 7 6 5 4 3 2 1

DYLAN WAS STILL AN EGG, but Ethel had already picked out her son's name. She hid him in a secret nest away from the hen house so Farmer would not collect him with the other eggs. Ethel had big plans for Dylan. If he ever got around to hatching.

But frankly, Ethel was tired of sitting on Dylan. He was hard and lumpy. She felt so stiff that she finally got up to take a little stretch.

"Anything yet?" asked her friends.

Ethel rolled her eyes. "Don't ask."

Cawly was an old crow who had lost a lot of feathers. He had gotten it into his head that eating a hen egg would make his feathers grow back.

While Ethel's back was turned, Cawly flapped down from the sweet gum tree and egg-napped Dylan.

"Cawly is stealing my son!" Ethel squawked. "Stop him!"

"Stop him yourself!" quacked Di the Duck who was sitting on her own lumpy eggs. "I'm busy here!"

Poor Ethel couldn't fly well. She ran around in circles, squawking, "Dylan! Mama's coming!" She flapped her wings until feathers flew in all directions. But she couldn't get ten feet off the ground.

Cawly heard all that racket behind him and figured that Ethel was hot on his tail. He flew to the top of a tall tree and dropped Dylan into a big nest. Then the old thief flapped off to the far side of the woods, feeling sorry for himself.

Ethel was frantic. She looked way up high at the huge nest and squawked her heart out.

"Dylan!" she cried. "Dylan! Dylan!"

Of course, Dylan didn't answer. He was an egg.

But the worst was yet to come.

At that moment, the owner of the nest returned home. She was an eagle whose name was too hard to pronounce. "Strange," she muttered to herself. "I remember these two fine eggs, but I do not recall this little one. I don't believe I've ever laid such a pitiful egg."

The situation was not good.
An eagle was sitting on Dylan.
Ethel was jumping up and down and squawking.

And Dylan picked that moment to hatch.

"Mama!" he cheeped.
"Son!" the eagle screamed.
Dylan was the sorriest-looking baby eagle she had ever seen.
"I will call you E-awk," she said. In the language of eagles,
E-awk means Ugly Little Runt.
But, of course, Dylan did not know that.
"I'll get food," she said. "You have a lot of growing to do."
Spreading her enormous wings, she flapped away.

Dylan looked over the side of the nest. Ethel was down there flapping around.

"Dylan!" she cried. "Dylan! It's you!"

"My name is E-awk!" he called down. "Who are you?"

"I'm your mother!" she called up.

"Then why am I up here, and you're down there?"

Ethel rolled her eyes. "Don't ask!"

The eagle returned with a great rush of wings.

"Who were you talking to?" she screamed.

"My mother," said Dylan.

"I'm your mother!" screamed the eagle whose name was too hard to pronounce.

"See? I brought you a nice plump rat!"

One of the other eggs cracked open and out popped
a girl eagle.

"If I look like that," thought Dylan, "I sure am ugly!"

"Oh, goody!" screamed the girl eagle. "A rat! I'm starved!"

The other egg cracked open and out tumbled a boy eagle.

"Give me that rat!" he screamed.

"I saw it first!" the girl eagle screamed.

They pecked at each other and fought over the rat.

Dylan hid behind the mother eagle.

"Who's that?" screamed the boy eagle.

"That's your brother!" screamed the mother eagle.

The boy eagle sniffed Dylan.

"You smell good!" he screamed. "I want to eat you!"

The mother eagle sniffed Dylan, too. "He does smell
good," she screamed. "Sort of like chicken. But he's still
your brother. You must not eat him. That's final." Then she
flew off after more food.

"I'm going to eat him!" screamed the boy eagle.

"I'll tell if you do!" screamed his sister.

Their mother came back and threw a snake into the nest.

"Fight over that!" she screamed.

Dylan dived under some sticks and hid.

"E-awk, you have to eat!" the mother eagle screamed. "What do you like?"

"I don't know!" Dylan screamed. "I'm only a baby!"

Muttering to herself, the mother eagle flew off.

"Are you really my mama?" Dylan called down to Ethel.

"Yes, Dylan," she called up.

"Then what do I eat? I'm hungry!"

"I'll send you up some nice corn!"

A sparrow named Sue carried five kernels of corn up to Dylan.

"What's that?" the boy eagle screamed.

"Corn!" Dylan screamed.

"Smells awful!" screamed the boy eagle.

"I'm going to tell!" screamed the girl eagle.

The mother eagle returned. She brought a bug for Dylan and a fish for the others.

"I'm not hungry," Dylan said.

"He ate corn!" screamed the girl eagle.

"Corn?" screamed the mother eagle. "Corn? I don't understand kids these days!"

Time passed, and all the children grew. When feathers started coming in, things got pretty crowded.

"Look at me!" the boy eagle screamed.

He flapped his wings and nearly knocked Dylan out of the nest.

"I can fly and you can't!" he screamed.

It was true. Dylan's feathers were small. His wings were small, too.

The mother eagle frowned at Dylan's tiny wings. "E-awk," she said, "this comes from eating corn. Stay here. You are not ready to fly yet."

Dylan watched the others sail away. They were whirling and diving through the air.

"You're scared to fly!" the boy eagle screamed at him. "You're too chicken!"

"Mama?" Dylan called down.

"Dylan?" she called up.

"Why can't I fly?"

"You can fly," she told him. "You can fly like a chicken. You just can't fly like an eagle. Fly down here!"

"I'm afraid!" he cried.

Right then two things happened that changed history.
One was that Arnold the Fox popped out of the woods
and headed for the hen house.

"It's Arnold!" the hens all squawked.

"Get the chicks into the coop!"

Chickens and chicks dashed from everywhere. In one big
flutter they dived into the hen house.

"I hate when that happens!" Arnold snarled.

Then he spotted Ethel. She had not run to save herself
with the others. She could not leave her son alone up there
in that eagle nest. She had stayed right there at the foot of
the tree.

Arnold smacked his lips.

"Lunch is served," he said with a smile.

That was when the second thing happened that changed history.

Dylan tried to fly. He jumped over the side of the nest and fell like a rock. He smacked the trunk and kept falling. He bounced off branches and fell and fell all the way down from the top of the tree.

"Look out below!" he screamed.

Arnold had already grabbed Ethel.

"I'm coming, Mama!" Dylan screamed, and he flapped his wings as hard as he could.

Arnold had never seen a chicken dive-bomb him from the top of a tree. Especially one screaming like an eagle!

MAMAA

"I'm out of here!" he yelped. He dropped Ethel and shot off for parts unknown.

Dylan made a perfect landing beside his mother. Ethel had never been so proud.

Every chicken in the hen house rushed out to crowd around Dylan. "How did you learn to scream like that?" clucked a boy chicken.

"What's your name?" clucked a girl chicken.

"E-awk," said Dylan.

"Oh, sure!" clucked the boy chicken. "That's an eagle's name!"

The mother eagle, whose name was too hard to pronounce, had watched Dylan drive away Arnold the Fox. She and her children swooped out of the sky and landed beside the chickens, which caused a whole new ruckus.

"E-awk!" screamed the mother eagle. "You did well!"

"Not bad for a chicken!" screamed the girl eagle.

"Come!" screamed the mother eagle to Dylan. "We must go!"

"Can I take a snack with me?" screamed the boy eagle.

"I can't go with you," Dylan told the mother eagle. "In my heart I'm a chicken. This is where I belong."

The mother eagle looked at E-awk for a long time. "Very well," she said. "Stay here if you must. We will not eat your friends. If that fox comes back, we'll eat him instead."

The eagles flew off faster than a cluck. The chickens all flapped their wings and crowed.

"You're a hero, E-awk!" the girl chicken clucked. "But your name is too hard to pronounce."

Dylan flapped his small wings and felt glad. "My name," he said, "is Dylan. From now on, I'm going to be Dylan."

And that is the story of how Dylan turned into an eagle and then turned into a chicken.